SUBIRA SUBIRA

by TOLOLWA M. MOLLEL • illustrated by LINDA SAPORT

CLARION BOOKS • NEW YORK

Clarion Books
a Houghton Mifflin Company imprint
215 Park Avenue South, New York, NY 10003
Text copyright © 2000 by Tololwa M. Mollel
Illustrations copyright © 2000 by Linda Saport
First Clarion paperback edition, 2006.

The illustrations were executed in pastel.
The text was set in 17-point Garamond.

www.houghtonmifflinbooks.com

Printed in Singapore.

Library of Congress Cataloging-in-Publication Data

Mollel, Tololwa M. (Tololwa Marti)
Subira subira / by Tololwa M. Mollel ; illustrations by Linda Saport.
p.   cm.
Summary: Set in contemporary Tanzania, this variation on a traditional tale describes
how a young girl learns a lesson in patience when a spirit woman sends her to
get three whiskers from a lion.
ISBN: 0-395-91809-X
[1. Folklore.] I. Saport, Linda, ill. II. Title.
PZ8.1.M73 Su   2000
[398.22]—dc21   98022564
CIP
AC

CL ISBN–13: 978-0-395-91809-8   CL ISBN–10: 0-395-91809-X
PA ISBN–13: 978-0-618-68926-2   PA ISBN–10: 0-618-68926-5

TWP 10 9 8 7 6 5 4

In memory of my father,
Loilang'isho Lotasarwaki
—T. M. M.

For Christian and Kelsey
—L. S.

One night, a few months after Mother died, Father said to Tatu, "Starting tomorrow, I'll be going to work early and returning late every day. I want you to take care of your little brother before and after school." He turned to Maulidi, who had been difficult lately. "Don't cause your sister any trouble."

But the very next morning, after Father had pedaled away on his rusty old bicycle, trouble started.

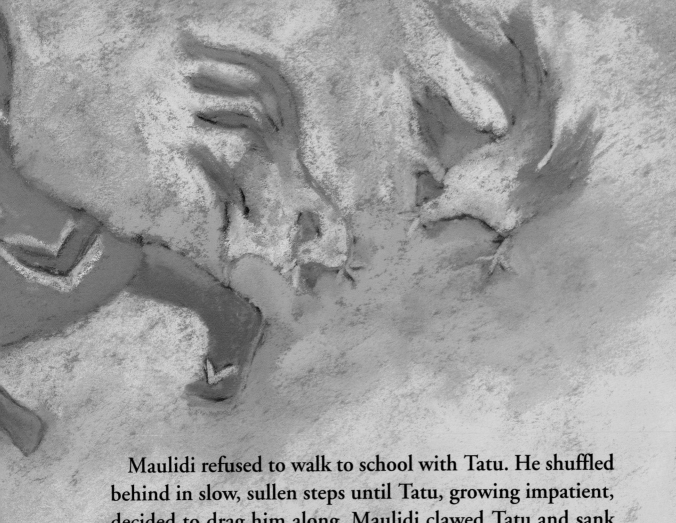

Maulidi refused to walk to school with Tatu. He shuffled behind in slow, sullen steps until Tatu, growing impatient, decided to drag him along. Maulidi clawed Tatu and sank his teeth into her arm. Angrily, Tatu grabbed him and shook him hard, until he cried and other school children stopped to pull them apart.

At home after school, Maulidi refused to do chores. "Don't tell me what to do," he snapped when Tatu tried to make him help fetch water from the stream. He tore himself away and threw rocks at her. Dodging the rocks, Tatu caught up with him. She wrestled him to the ground, and neighbors had to separate them.

8

When Father returned home that night, Tatu showed
him her bandaged arm and complained bitterly about
Maulidi. Father sighed wearily. "I'll deal with him when he
wakes up tomorrow."

In the morning before he left, Father gave Maulidi a
sound scolding. And over the next few days, he dealt
sternly with him. But it didn't help. Maulidi's fights with
Tatu only got worse. "I don't know what else to do about
him," Father grumbled to Tatu one night.

Tatu, however, knew just what to do.

The next day, she went to the forest to look for MaMzuka, a mysterious spirit woman who lived there and granted wishes.

"To see MaMzuka," Mother had once told Tatu, "one has to be a good singer. MaMzuka loves a good song."

Tatu graced the forest with her voice.

Subira, subira subira, subira
Subira nikuone, subira
MaMzuka tafadhali, subira
Subira, subira subira, subira.

An ugly, croaking voice behind Tatu made her jump. "You sing as magically as your mother when she came to see me years ago." Before Tatu, leaning on a staff, stood a hideous old woman.

The woman's bony hand gripped Tatu. "Give me a little snuff and I'll listen to your wish!" she ordered.

Tatu knew how much MaMzuka liked snuff and had brought some in a little bottle. MaMzuka tucked a pinch of snuff under her lower lip and carefully stashed the bottle in her gown pocket.

Then, with her long staff, MaMzuka tapped a nearby tree trunk. It opened into a strange dark house lit with tiny birds' eggs.

Sitting at a little table inside, Tatu told MaMzuka all about her brother and their terrible fights. "I wish you would make him good," she pleaded. "I don't want to hurt him. And I don't want him to hurt me again."

"I can grant many wishes," MaMzuka said, "but only you can turn your brother into someone better."

"How?" Tatu asked.

"Tonight, when the world is asleep," replied MaMzuka, "go out, unseen and unheard, to the clearing with the giant anthill. There you will find a lion. From the lion, pluck three whiskers and bring them to me."

Tatu gasped. "A lion? A lion's whiskers!"

MaMzuka stood up. "Your courage and patience will guide you," she said mysteriously, and the next moment she vanished.

That night, as the world slept, Tatu slipped out of the house, unseen and unheard. She knew the clearing MaMzuka had mentioned. She and Maulidi used to play at the giant anthill every Saturday.

Tatu walked along the moonlit path. The wind danced on trees. Weeds rustled. Soon she came to the clearing.

From the anthill a massive lion watched her, swaying his powerful tail. Tatu shook with terror, but she remembered MaMzuka's words and calmed herself.

Ignoring the sullen stare of the lion, she inched forward
and sang:

> *Subira, subira subira, subira*
> *Subira nijongee, subira*
> *Nduli tafadhali, subira*
> *Subira, subira subira, subira.*

The lion seemed to be spellbound. But as Tatu reached
the anthill, he growled.

Tatu continued to sing and slowly retreated. Heading home, she wished she had been bolder. "But I'll be patient," she told herself, remembering MaMzuka's words.

The next night, hoping the lion would be there, Tatu returned to the anthill. She found him in the same spot, and sang as she advanced.

This time, before the lion snapped out of her spell, Tatu got all the way to the top of the hill.

On the third night, Tatu climbed the hill and knelt beside the lion. Still singing, she stroked and groomed his mane.

Subira, subira subira, subira
Subira nikufume, subira
Nduli tafadhali, subira
Subira, subira subira, subira.

The lion fell asleep.
Tatu plucked three whiskers and placed them in a little tin.

21

As Tatu sang for MaMzuka the next day after school, her mind buzzed with curiosity. Just what would MaMzuka do with the whiskers?

When MaMzuka appeared, Tatu handed her the tin. MaMzuka opened it. Then, to Tatu's dismay, she blew the whiskers away.

"You've thrown them away!" Tatu exclaimed. "You told me I needed the whiskers to change my brother!"

"You don't need them," said MaMzuka. "To change your brother, just remember how you got the whiskers."

Without another word, MaMzuka vanished into the green of the forest.

Walking back home, Tatu thought over what MaMzuka had told her. She thought about it as she did the chores, and all evening until she went to bed.

On the way to school in the morning, when Maulidi dragged his feet, Tatu remembered how she had obtained the whiskers, and didn't fight her brother.

Much as she wanted to!

Instead, she ignored him, the same way she had the sullen stare of the lion, and began to sing a song. Tatu knew how much Maulidi used to enjoy Mother's singing. She hoped he would sing along and walk faster to school. He didn't. Nonetheless, Tatu felt very proud of herself that she didn't have a fight with him.

At home after school, she had a pleasant surprise. Maulidi, smiling, asked her to teach him the song.

Tatu smiled back. "Only if you promise to hurry to school tomorrow."

That speeded up Maulidi the next morning.

Singing and dancing, he arrived at school alongside Tatu.

But the rest of Maulidi's day didn't go as well. After school, sulking, he climbed a tree and wouldn't come down.

Ignoring him, Tatu danced home, singing another new song.

When Maulidi finally came home, Tatu offered to teach him the song. "But only if you help me fetch water," she added. "I'll race you to the stream."

Tatu was scooping water into her bucket when Maulidi, half-willing, arrived at the stream.

On Saturday morning, Tatu offered to teach Maulidi yet
another song. "But only if you come with me to the
anthill," she said.

For the first time in weeks, Tatu and Maulidi set off to
play at the anthill. Father looked up from fixing his bicycle
to wish them a good time. Tatu could tell he was surprised
and pleased.

28

When they returned home, a tired Maulidi lay down to take a nap after lunch. Watching at his bedside, Tatu wished Maulidi were always as nice as he had been that morning. "But I'll be patient," Tatu told herself. "Patient, just like taming the lion." Then, as she had seen Mother do many times, she sang Maulidi to sleep.

Subira, subira subira, subira
Subira nikulaze, subira
Maulidi tafadhali, subira
Subira, subira subira, subira.

31

AUTHOR'S NOTE

This is an adaptation of a folk tale, found in Africa and Asia, about a woman seeking to win the affection of her husband, or, in some versions, her stepson. A wise man advises her to get the whiskers of a lion (in Asia, a tiger) to help her accomplish the task. The woman finds the beast and through patience wins it over with food and obtains the whiskers. I've made my version more child-centered than the traditional tale and have set it in contemporary Tanzania. The characters have been modified accordingly, and I've introduced a Swahili song as part of the story's new orientation. For the song, I borrowed a tune from one of the many story songs I learned while growing up in Tanzania.

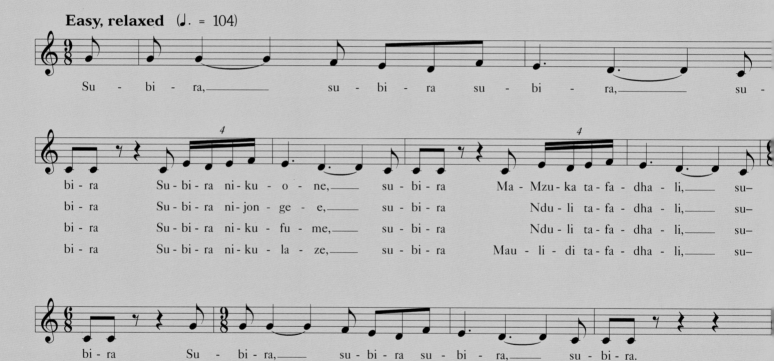

Easy, relaxed (♩. = 104)

Su - bi - ra,_____ su - bi - ra su - bi - ra,_____ su-

bi - ra Su - bi - ra ni - ku - o - ne,_____ su - bi - ra Ma - Mzu - ka ta - fa - dha - li,_____ su—
bi - ra Su - bi - ra ni - jon - ge - e,_____ su - bi - ra Ndu - li ta - fa - dha - li,_____ su—
bi - ra Su - bi - ra ni - ku - fu - me,_____ su - bi - ra Ndu - li ta - fa - dha - li,_____ su—
bi - ra Su - bi - ra ni - ku - la - ze,_____ su - bi - ra Mau - li - di ta - fa - dha - li,_____ su—

bi - ra Su - bi - ra,_____ su - bi - ra su - bi - ra,_____ su - bi - ra.

Transcribed by Paul Alan Lev

MaMzuka (mum ZOO kah): Spirit Woman • **Maulidi** (ma OO lee dee): a Tanzanian boy's name • **nduli** (nn DOO lee): lion • **nijongee** (nee john GEH EH): let me draw close • **nikufume** (nee KOO foo meh): let me braid your hair (mane) • **nikulaze** (nee KOO la zeh): let me get you to sleep • **nikuone** (nee KOO oh neh): let me see you • **subira** (soo BEE rah): patience, or a call to be understanding, tolerant, or calm • **tafadhali** (tah fah THUH lee): please • **Tatu** (TAH too): a Tanzanian girl's name